CHRIST'S JOURNAL

BOOKS BY

PAUL ALEXANDER BARTLETT

NOVELS

VOICES FROM THE PAST:
Sappho's Journal • Christ's Journal • Leonardo da Vinci's Journal
Shakespeare's Journal • Lincoln's Journal

When the Owl Cries

Adiós Mi México

Forward, Children!

POETRY

Wherehill

Spokes for Memory

NONFICTION

The Haciendas of Mexico: An Artist's Record

CHRIST'S JOURNAL

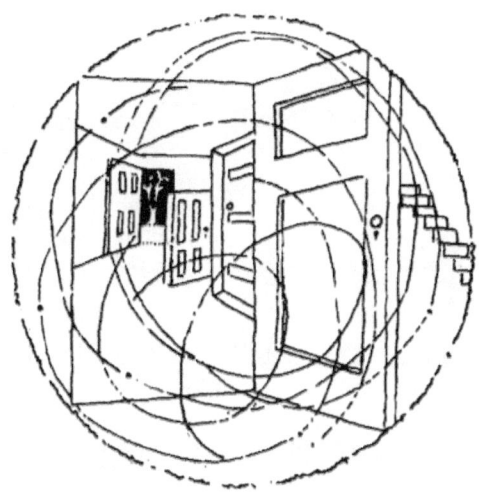

by
PAUL ALEXANDER BARTLETT
and
Illustrated by the Author

Edited by
STEVEN JAMES BARTLETT

AUTOGRAPH EDITIONS
Salem, Oregon

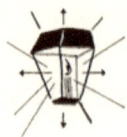

AUTOGRAPH EDITIONS
P. O. Box 6141 · Salem, Oregon 97304

ᛰ Established 1975 ᛱ

Copyright © 2007 by Steven James Bartlett
First Edition

ISBN 978-0-6151-5645-3

Library of Congress Catalog Card Number: 2006025662

Printed in the United States of America

Library of Congress Cataloguing-in-Publication Data

Bartlett, Paul Alexander.
  Christ's journal / by Paul Alexander Bartlett and illustrated by the author ;
edited by Steven James Bartlett. -- 1st ed.
    p. cm.
  Summary: "A historical novel that recounts the last months of Christ's life
from an autobiographical perspective"--Provided by publisher.
  ISBN 978-0-6151-5645-3
  1. Jesus Christ--Fiction. I. Bartlett, Steven J. II. Title.

PS3602.A8396C46 2006
813'.6--dc22
                                                        2006028950

CONTENTS

PREFACE

Steven James Bartlett

Senior Research Professor of Philosophy, Oregon State University
and
Visiting Scholar in Psychology & Philosophy, Willamette University

*C*hrist's Journal is one of five independent works of fiction which together make up *Voices from the Past*, a quintet of novels that describe the inner lives of five extraordinary people. Progressing through time from the most distant to the most recent they are: Sappho of Lesbos, the famous Greek poet; Jesus; Leonardo da Vinci; Shakespeare; and Abraham Lincoln. For the most part, little is known about the inward realities of these people, about their personal thoughts, reflections, and the quality and nature of their feelings. For this reason they have become no more than voices from the past: The contributions they have left us remain, but little remains of each person, of his or her personality, of the loves, fears, pleasures, hatreds, beliefs, and thoughts each had.

Voices from the Past was written by Paul Alexander Bartlett over a period of several decades. After his death in an automobile accident in 1990, the manuscripts of the five novels were discovered among his as yet unpublished papers. He had been at work adding the finishing touches to the manuscripts. Now, more than a decade and a half after his death, the publication of *Voices from the Past* is overdue.

Bartlett is known for his fiction, including *When the Owl Cries* and *Adiós Mi México*, historical novels set during the Mexican Revolution of 1910 and descriptive of hacienda life, *Forward, Children!*, a powerful antiwar novel, and numerous short stories. He was also the author of books of poetry, including *Spokes for Memory* and *Wherehill*, the nonfiction work, *The Haciendas of Mexico: An Artist's Record*, the first extensive artistic and photographic study of haciendas throughout Mexico, and numerous articles about the Mexican haciendas. Bartlett was also an artist whose paintings, illustrations, and drawings have been exhibited in more than 40 one-man shows in leading museums in the U.S. and Mexico.

Archives of his work and literary correspondence have now been established at the American Heritage Center of the University of Wyoming, the Nettie Lee Benson Latin American Collection of the University of Texas, and the Rare Books Collection of the University of California, Los Angeles.

Paul Alexander Bartlett's life was lived with a single value always central: a sustained dedication to beauty, which he believed was the most vital value of living and his reason for his life as a writer and an artist. *Voices from the Past* reflects this commitment, for he believed that these five voices, in their different ways, express a passion for life, for the creative spirit, and ultimately for beauty in a variety of its forms—poetic and natural (Sappho), spiritual (Jesus), scientific and artistic (da Vinci), literary (Shakespeare), and humanitarian (Lincoln). In this work, he has sought, as faithfully as possible, to relay across time a renewed lyrical meaning of these remarkable individuals, lending them his own voice, with a mood, simplicity, depth of feeling, and love of beauty that were his, and, he believed, also theirs.

The journal form has been used only rarely in works of fiction. Bartlett believed that as a form of literature the journal offers the most effective way to bring back to life the life-worlds of significant, unique, highly individual, and important creators. In each of the novels that make up *Voices from the Past,* his interest is to portray the inner experience of exceptional and special people, about whom there is scant knowledge on this level. During the many years of research he devoted to a study of the lives and thoughts of Sappho, Jesus, Leonardo, Shakespeare, and Lincoln, he sought to base the journals on what is known and what can be surmised about the person behind each voice, and he wove into each journal passages from their writings and the substance of the testimony of others. Yet the five novels are fiction: They re-express in an author's creation lives now buried by the passage of centuries.

I am deeply grateful to my wife, Karen Bartlett, for her faithful, patient, and perceptive help with this long project.

✧

For my father,
Paul Alexander Bartlett,
whose kindness, love of beauty and of place
will always be greatly missed.

CHRIST'S JOURNAL

$\mathcal{T}$he sun is setting. The evening is very warm. Across the fields I hear children's voices as they play.

This evening I have been reading the *Psalms* and their beauty fills my mind. I have decided to write my thoughts, not because I am a psalmist, but because I hope to get closer to the meaning of life. Of course I should have started writing long ago. When I was in the wilderness I had an opportunity. Now, it is hard for me to find the time, and writing is not a habit of mine and does not come easily.

However, like a shepherd, I shall gather together my thoughts, watching for strays. In spite of vigilance my thoughts may wander.

It is pleasant sitting here at this table, the night air blowing in; a star is caught in a tree. Peter is talking to a friend; Peter's voice has always pleased me, so deep.

Elul 20

Yesterday, when I was in Naim, someone pointed out a sick man huddled in rags at a street corner. It was one of those windy days and dust spun around us. The man reached up his arms and mumbled; I remembered seeing him before and maybe he remembered me. I felt his hope; I felt I could help, and I said:

"Pick up your mat, get up...walk... God will help you."

The fellow trembled. He seemed to shrink inside himself as if afraid of me. He closed his eyes and doubled his hands. I waited and then repeated my command slowly. Like someone in a dream he untangled his rags and knelt. As he rolled his mat I encouraged him. Glancing about furtively, he stood, tottered. I thought he would fall but he kept his eyes on mine and I urged him to walk.

"Master...master," he muttered, staring about uncertainly. "Master...where...

how can I?"

Limping, carrying his mat under one arm, he headed for the synagogue and as I watched he began to walk easily. He threw down his mat and began to run. Dust swirled around us and he disappeared from sight.

Later, someone told me he had been bedridden, crippled for almost forty years. Forty years—he had been crippled longer than I had lived! Now he was walking...running... I felt such joy, such joy, all day. I couldn't eat when I sat at the table at Peter's; his mother scolded me. To please her I nibbled a little fruit. I couldn't find anyone who could share my joy so I walked alone, roamed the countryside. As I walked I could see his tortured face, dirty beard, beggar's clothes. Forty years...

His name is Simeon.

Probably I will see Simeon soon. And what shall I say when he thanks me? What can he say? I will see a changed man and that will be enough.

*I*t seems only yesterday I was in Nazareth yet that yesterday was years ago. Regardless of the passage of time I feel the summer heat and hear flies buzzing. Father is at work in his shop. Whitey comes to me and meows; she's scared of the thunder rumbling in the distance; she's hungry too. Mama is cooking and the smell of beef is everywhere.

Father begins to saw and sawdust spills over his feet. I lean against a wall and sunshine spreads and I feel everything impregnate me, the stucco, earth floor, the bench, the broken handle of the saw, Father batting flies that try to settle on his beard. This will last forever. Caught in the web of time we will eat supper together, before lamp lighting, and Whitey will sit on my lap.

I recall another afternoon years ago—the same place. But Father is upset, talking volubly, denouncing Herod and his tyranny, an old, old story for all of us. I have tried to deny the truth of that story but there it is, Herod's soldiers slaughtering innocent children, hoping to kill me. Surely I hate the man and yet I have learned to pity his blundering.

As a boy I wandered, praying, asking understanding. The dry hills were uncommunicative. If it is impossible to forgive it is possible to look ahead. I felt too that my guilt might become a disease. I saw that the past can have too powerful an influence.

Tomorrow I am to preach on a hill... Peter says the weather will be fine. I hope so, after windy days. For weeks we have had wind and cold.

Here, in my room at Peter's, I am discontented. The windows try to send me outdoors. They face cornfields and the corn is waist high, brown and roughly swaying. I wish I could stretch out in the middle of a field, lie there and watch the clouds and listen to the wind. I am happiest when outdoors.

The sun is down but I won't light my candle; instead, I'll watch the coming night and perhaps I can summon thoughts for tomorrow; perhaps something will talk to me in the cornfields, something I can impart. Friends and strangers will arrive tomorrow...

Darkness has taken over and I can barely see to write...a cricket speaks...may profound thoughts come.

I spoke to them on a little hill, a rocky place. It wasn't windy or hot and we were not troubled by flies and as I stood before them, fishermen, villagers, friends and strangers, sitting on rocks and on the ground, on shawls and blankets, I was deeply moved. I was specially moved by an old woman near me who never took her eyes off me. Dressed in blue, her clothes in tatters, her face gleamed. Wrinkled cheeks were kind. There was kindness in her folded hands, but, most of all, it was the compassion in her eyes, soft, tearful, blue eyes, that had searched for so long and hoped for so long. Hers was the patience of the poor. Her spirit became my spirit as I talked.

"Blessed are the poor...for theirs is the kingdom of heaven. You are the salt of the earth—you are the light of the world. Let your light so shine before men that they may see your good works and glorify your Father in heaven.

"Blessed are the meek," I said, "for they shall inherit the earth. Blessed are they that mourn for they shall be comforted...blessed are those who hunger after justice...blessed are the merciful for they shall obtain mercy."

The old woman had buried her face in her hands: she was my mother and every mother, sincerity and love, the symbol of integrity.

A breeze came and white clouds piled along the horizon. The crowd increased and the hill was covered with people. Shepherds approached and held their flocks in check, listening.

"...Rejoice and be exceedingly glad," I said to them, "...yours is the strength of thousands...yours is the strength of the chosen, the humble and the contrite, the pure and lowly...blessed are the lowly. Be ye perfect, even as your Father who is in heaven..."

I tried to express my sincerity, the sincerity that began in the desert, that has been accumulating, that is, for me, the essence of living. I tried to speak slowly, measuring each word. By the time I was finished I was very tired. I was glad to feel Peter's hand on my arm and hear him ask:

"Aren't you hungry?"

A lamb blundered against my legs and I stooped and picked it up and held it in my arms, thinking of my humble birth. There was such comfort, holding it; I felt my strength return. I thought of the stable in Bethlehem. When I went to see it years ago nothing remained but a watering trough and a fence. Time had also swept away the star and the Magi.

Men, women and children pressed around me, talking, praising, asking questions. When I put down the lamb it dashed away. Questions—there is no end to questions. I am glad and yet I am world-weary. World thoughts oppressed me. The moon was well up before I could get away and walk to Peter's; as we bowed our heads at the table someone knocked on the door.

Tishri 21

Sometimes people say I am an unhappy man.

That is not true.

For one thing, I like to remember happy experiences, and one of them was the wedding at Cana. What a pleasant stroll it was, the day temperate, the path climbing gradually above palm trees of the valley, up to the vineyards. Birds were gossiping in the vineyards. The blue of the Jordan flashed through oleanders. The snowy top of Hermon sent out a string of flamingos.

At Cana, Mother greeted me. There were old friends among the guests. Miriam was beautiful, more beautiful than I remembered. I thought of Solomon's song as I watched her, "Thou art in the clefts of the rock; let me see thy countenance, let me hear thy voice, for sweet is thy voice and thy countenance is comely..."

After we had eaten Mother came to me and said "there is no more wine... Miriam is distressed...a wedding without wine!" she exclaimed, gesturing toward the guests at their outdoor tables. Certainly it was Miriam's day. I thought of our friendship through the years and I decided to change water into wine, a token to their youth and their happiness.

I called two of the servants.

"Fill the water pots with water...now empty them into the wine pitchers. There will be wine for everyone."

"It's good wine," I heard someone remark.

Miriam thanked me and I hoped for acceptance on the part of everyone. A beginning has been made, perhaps a seal or symbol had been placed on my ministry. I tasted the wine on my lips as I walked to Peter's. Before I had gone any distance Andrew and Phillip criticized the miracle. They said I could change a man's soul as easily. They were afraid. Mother, walking with us, defended me and ridiculed them.

Alone, I struck out across a grain field where men were dismantling a tent; behind a stick fence donkeys brayed; day was closing behind its fence of clouds; I felt that the men dismantling their tent were also dismantling time.

Alone, the happiness of the wedding returned.

I tasted the wine.

*F*ather is too old to work and I want him to sell one of the Magi gifts, help himself and Mother. This has been a poor carpentry season for him and for others. No use has been made of the gifts these years but he won't listen. He will not so much as hint where they are stored. Where else but the synagogue? He is afraid of the wealth, of robbers...

It is easy to get him started about the Magi. His eyebrow cocks, his head tilts, he pulls his beard and settles himself, legs crossed. He describes camels, accoutrements, attendants, a long, long story, growing longer with the years. The star and the angels are always there. He becomes eloquent like someone who had dabbled in divination.

"Casper...Melchior...Balthasar..."

Mother is pronouncing their names. She is fondest of the Babylonian king.

"He was tall and stately and wore a dark blue robe. His hair and beard were snowy white..."

It was a harsh journey into Egypt, some of the time without water, the heat so overpowering they walked at night. At an encampment, Egyptian soldiers provided food while Mother rested a few days. A sergeant repaired her sandals. They followed an ancient caravan route, asking for help. They lived with Gabra nomads—borrowing a white camel, a day or two. Father says "she was a real princess on that camel!" They hid in a hutment from Herod's men, his troops passing on maneuvers. A lone traveler gave them dates and bread. They begged eggs at a caravanserai...a little goat's milk...a little meat.

Mother praised her donkey. He never refused to carry her. For a while they stopped under sycamores where it was cool, a pond nearby. But they were very hungry. There, under the trees, the donkey died. They thought they would never get back to Israel. Father had the Magi gifts sewn to the donkey's pad but when the animal died he had to carry everything. Utterly disheartened, they trudged on. They got lost. There were sand storms.

Mother begged him to sell the gold cup. "It's not mine to sell," he objected. But he traded Melchior's coins, "for the sake of our boy." So they survived. Herod's men continued to haunt them; then they learned that he was dead.

"Despicable men do despicable things," Father said. "Rome is the great instigator of crimes. The *Kittim*! Political schemes are hatched in the Forum with the wild beasts. Rome appoints a governor for Jerusalem; the man is in exile so he devours us, his subjects."

Last night I lay awake most of the night, haunted by these ghosts. The past can be a simoom. Maybe it is a good thing when today's problems wipe out yesterday's problems. When the oil in the lamp burned out I tried to find oil in the storage shed. There was no more. At dawn I read my favorite psalms.

A thousand hoplites marched through our town. Drums. Horns. Thud of spears.

Many people fled.

Last month the hoplites caused a riot in Naim.

I am unable to countenance such hirelings. I am unable to countenance military death.

Friends are still troubled by my miracle at Cana. As a group of us walked to Jerusalem their annoyance went on and on.

In Jerusalem I was annoyed by the bellowing of cattle, the bleating of sacrificial sheep. An ox screamed. Dust rose from underfoot as I jostled turbaned men... A woman in a striped veil blocked my way.

Passing Herod's temple I searched for sky. Men had worked for years to build that temple—was it for dust and smoke?

At the temple I stood among money exchange tables and listened to men haggle. A strange, dark, bestial man lorded over everyone. At an ivory-topped table men quarreled and spat. A sacrificial trumpet shrilled. I grabbed my *taliss*, the one Father gave me. Knotting it into a whip I struck the money from a table.

Coins spun. An exchanger howled. I lashed another table, upset it, then another. A crowd jeered as I demanded that they honor the temple.

"This is man's place of worship. You offend God. Look, what you're doing... take your money away...you know our temple is sacred. God's temple is a temple of peace."

Later, when a judge demanded an explanation, I saw my own disrespect, my own violence. He was a lanky, stone-like figure, grey-haired, grey-faced, palsied. He understood my rebellion, the rankling perturbations of my life.

"I'm a Greek," he said. "I realize your alienation. I'm new here. I have much to learn. When a man revolts there is usually well-grounded reason. But be careful! The next time there may be fines or punishment; another man may not be lenient."

Heshvan 9

That night, after scourging the temple, I dreamed of home: I was working at the carpenter's bench, making a three-legged stool. I finished smoothing the legs and sat on the floor, Whitey beside me. She was playing with a heap of shavings.

Again I had that illusion that time was mine, that the sunshine and flies and smell of olive oil and earth would never leave me. And I thought, as I worked on the stool, how pleased Mother would be when I finished it for her birthday. I glanced at a mark on the wall and wondered if I had grown taller.

Galilee

A storm. The lake. Two fishermen drowned. Tents blown over. Next day as I bury the dead a little girl comes and throws herself at my feet, a flower clutched in her hand. What does death mean to her?

Heshvan 11

Wearing dirty work clothes I was readily admitted into the prison at

Machaerus, a citadel high above the countryside. Guards shrugged as I entered. A door clanged with a terrible crash: I was in John's cell. Kissing me, hugging me, we embraced: as always I felt he was part of me.

"How are you, cousin? I thought we would never get to see each other again...in all those rags they didn't know you. You chose a good time; there has been an ugly quarrel going on...we have new guards. Here, here, sit by me."

John has been imprisoned five months and is chained to the wall, a loop around one leg, letting him move a few feet. Rattling the chain, he nodded and grinned at me. I did not understand what he whispered. When he was certain we were alone he grasped his chain and forced it open, first one link and then another. Though he had been a wrestler and farmer I was amazed. Free, he clasped me in his arms.

"It's a great trick...nobody knows...I can get up at night and walk around... maybe there's a way to get out of here."

How often we have been taken for brothers because of our red hair; we trim our beards the same way; our faces are much alike except that mine is leaner. We were brothers as we talked, sitting on the stone floor, the chain between us.

John urged me to leave Capernaum.

"You can't go on preaching there. Antipas has men on the lookout for you. He's as cruel as Herod, you know that! Go in hiding for a while, Jesus. There's no good in it if both of us end up in chains. Our ministry will fail."

I had concealed bread and fruit in my clothes but John would not eat while I was there. I gave him a comb and he combed his beard and head, grimacing, laughing. I asked him to change clothes with me: "You can put me in chains," I said.

An empty cell, stone walls, chains, the Dead Sea glistening dozens of feet below, a cold floor, a little food...what could I do?

"Are there other prisoners on this floor, John?"

"I never see them... I'm not allowed outside."

"You know that we are trying to free you."

"Don't run any risks."

"We aren't afraid."

"I have enough to eat...time to pray."

"We need you."

He bowed in prayer.

To be born anew...that is our hope for mankind.

I went away embittered. Think of it, I left a comb and some bread and fruit for a great man, a man of God. As I walked through the night I heard and re-heard those words:

"May the Lord bless thee and keep thee, the Lord make His face to shine upon thee and be gracious unto thee; the Lord lift up His countenance and give thee peace."

Peace inside stone walls.

When shall John and I meet again?

Peter's
Heshvan 19

I have preached in the synagogues at Cana and Capernaum during the last few days. I do not like preaching indoors. The sky is best and weeds and grass make the best floor. Old laws become new laws outdoors. I stress repentance and faith—the time is now at hand. I try to speak with authority and yet avoid rigid precepts.

Usually I walk alone. Being alone, from time to time, is essential: there is a peace in the company of one's own shadow. After every meeting I am again surrounded by questioners, most of them respectful, some are quite idle and oblivious of anything but themselves.

At Capernaum, as I spoke, swallows flew in and out, swooping low. I wondered, as I watched them, are we the interlopers, have we usurped their place? For me birds epitomize the highest form of beauty.

Near Capernaum I met an officer as I rested under trees along the road. His horse was lathered with sweat and the man was tired; he leaned forward in the saddle and eyed me critically, in silence. I asked him to dismount and rest.

Joining me he said he had heard of my miracle at the wedding and my cure of the street beggar. He brushed dust off his immaculate uniform. Wiping his face he scrutinized me, then pled with me to come and heal his son who was, according to his doctor, dying of fever. I shared fruit and he introduced himself; he admitted he had sought me as a last resort. I pitied the young father, fond of his only child, yet so skeptical. Rising nervously, catching his horse's bridle, he urged me to go to his home.

"I can't wait any longer... You don't seem to understand that my son is dying. Ride to Capernaum. Take my horse. Ride...help my boy. Master, cure him...he has been ill with a terrible fever...for days... I must find help if you can't help..."

"Ride home," I said. "Your son will live; from this very hour he will improve. Ride home in peace...do not hurry... God has answered your plea, our prayers."

I felt my faith attend the boy as he lay in bed. For a little while he became my son—the son I would never have. I blessed him. My faith, God's grace, would renew the child. My power was adequate. I did not need to travel to Capernaum.

Never looking back, the officer rode off, dubious, angry. A breeze clattered dry leaves above me.

I knelt in prayer.

I am troubled because there are so many sick in the world.

Capernaum...Capernaum...the village might be all mankind.

Here I healed the mother of my host, a woman gravely ill of seizures. I had hardly helped her and finished my dinner when people clamored at the door, the demented as well as the sick.

Still riding his bay, the officer found me and assured me his son was recovering—his ardent gratitude was so bewildering, so nervous. As we talked in the courtyard of my host's home people jostled him. He tried to send them away, to establish a sense of intimacy with me.

Walking through the town at dusk I touched this one, spoke to another. A sense of anonymity troubled me: it was everywhere. The exultant friends, the overjoyed crowd, forced me to retreat. As I closed the door of the house I observed Roman soldiers. I asked to be left alone. I ate supper alone. Early in the morning, shortly after dawn, I slipped away to the hills.

Peter's

Simeon came. We sat on stools and he thanked me, tears in his eyes. Clean, wearing new clothes, a little shawl around him, he related how thrilling it was to be able to move about, to "really walk." He explained what it had been to be "a stone in the street, a stone to spit on." Eyes burning, he made me know what it was to be forsaken, abused, hungry.

He says he has told others of his cure. Only a few mockers doubt. Friends and strangers visit his house, to touch him. He imitated poking hands. Simeon is a pathetically handsome man, still frail, his frailty accenting his features. "My cousin Ephriam has promised me a job," he said.

"I'm fifty-three but you've made me young. My memory is coming back. Everything tastes good..."

I believe my faith will help people because it is a faith of hope, a faith that conquers obstacles; it is a faith based on patience and kindness. We have no right to kill, no right to inflict pain. Ours is the gift of understanding, contentment. Ours is the honoring of simplicity and honesty.

Sun on the hills is a kind of faith...the vineyard that endures is another...the wounded heron struggling on...childbirth pain...fishermen drying their nets on the beach...

Our Father Who art in heaven, hallowed be Thy name...

He is our guide, Father of us all, brother of us all, master of all. Seek and you will find. Our kingdom is at hand.

I have been reading a scroll, an ancient one.

I write outdoors, on a table, under olives.

As I speak in public I become more and more a master of words. I detect the difference in just a month or so. I am encouraged. I no longer have to think what I do with my hands and arms, how I stand. Thoughts flow.

Going from place to place I see the same heads. The sun streams over us at the benediction. The passion of living is obvious, touching each of us, offering kinship and peace.

Salt of the earth...

John is the salt of the earth and yet he writes me that he has been beaten by his guards. Several times I have returned to Capernaum to visit Joseph, the young officer. He has promised to use his influence to free John. How wary he is of becoming involved with the prison authorities. In Jerusalem my intercessions are ridiculed: John is branded treasonous.

Authorities are evasive or antagonistic. They ridicule our wish to uplift the world. I am told to take care.

Guards at the citadel refused to allow me to visit John.

Written requests go unanswered.

Peter, James and Matthew are no luckier than I.

A finch is watching me as I write under the olives.

Rain is threatening.

Conception. Birth. Death. Each is a mystery.

In my father's house I grew up among mysteries. I heard them talked, argued over, curtly dismissed. I have resented the unknowns, yet to plumb them is still beyond me. Each child is a mystery. The temple is a mystery. The shell that I pick up on the beach has its mystery. Some say I am a man of mysteries. Does the turtle have its mysteries?

Kislev 5

For days I have been too busy and preoccupied to write—preaching often, healing often. I am writing in a borrowed tent; James and Mark are asleep inside.

Yesterday, on the lake shore, I was circled by a crowd. I talked to them till late. I wish to record the promises I made them:

> *Verily, I say unto you, he that believeth in me hath everlasting life. I am that bread of life. Your fathers ate manna in the wilderness, and are dead. I am living bread. If any man eat of this bread he shall live forever.*

In keeping with my promise I passed out bread and fish in baskets. I blessed the food and there was an abundance for everyone, many of them hungry children.

Mark and James and Phillip passed the baskets till each was fed, the fish and bread always sufficient. At parting I reminded the people of the deeper meaning but some were overwhelmed by the miracle. A youngster ran about shouting: "He made the bread...he made the fish...with his own hands. Jesus made..."

A strange restlessness troubled almost everyone.

Phillip, Andrew and I strolled along a white path, as white, in the moonlight, as if made of crushed shells. Galilee was flat and silvery. Andrew continued to comment about the "bread and fish" at almost every turn of the path. His youthful, enthusiastic face warned me, warned me that youth is irresponsible. What is the proper age for wisdom? As for miracles is there a miracle surpassing the miracle of faith?

Peter has made me a tent. It is dark green, and big enough for two. The tent pole is an antique shepherd's staff. A charioteer and a number of untranslatable characters have been carved on the wood.

"Papa gave me that staff long ago. He said it is Assyrian."

I can carry the tent comfortably and the staff is never out of my hands.

Peter's
Kislev 6

Last night I dreamed I was a tree—a cedar tree.
"Don't cut me down," I begged. "I am shade...I am the home of birds."
I sat underneath the tree and fell asleep. I slept inside a dream.

Peter's Home
Kislev 10

John is dead. Murdered.
He has been beheaded.
The world has lost a voice of reason. I have lost my best friend. He was beheaded at a drunken orgy—his head was displayed like a trophy at the palace. What desecration, abuse, folly, horror. I can barely write...sorrow...resentment... my mind whirls to the days we passed together in the desert, our wilderness comradeship. His faith was my faith. Our bonds were those of true brotherhood.

I should have been able to free him. Instead I gave him dried fruit and a comb. The letters I wrote did nothing. My petitions were disregarded. I was too patient. I have sat in this room all day...nothing has come of my sorrow but more sorrow. Peter and James and Mark have had their say.

Late in the evening friends arrived, wanting to plan his burial. Permission has been granted: we are to be permitted to claim his body. It is best to have the sacred privilege of farewell. We tell each other that we must succeed for his sake, man of poverty, prison and death.

For his sake we can burn our lamps and candles and share late communion, get up early, walk many leagues and extol his faith. We will tell it on the hills and in the towns and in the villages. I feel his wrestler's hand tighten on my shoulder.

Kislev 12

We brought John to the ancient rocky crypts, a dozen of us. Some of us wound scarves around our faces. Mother suspected that we were followed. She insisted on two to act as guards.

Simon was there... Matthew, Peter, Luke, Mark...they helped us lay John outside his crypt, helped us cut stone. A torch burned Mark's arm; someone smashed our hammer. "Work fast," someone was constantly urging. Peter got defiant: "Let the Romans come," he shouted. "We have a right to bury our dead." Luke had to calm him. It was dawn before we had the crypt sealed; we were cut and bruised. No torches.

As I sat among the cliff rocks I tried to obliterate the tragedy, tried to refute his death. Hard to breathe. Hard to utter the final prayer. Think of it...we had buried a headless man, friend, friend...

As we stole into town we met the *Kittim* officer, riding for Capernaum; he did not recognize me of course. What a stark figure! I wanted to talk to him about his son but Mother begged me: we must not trust him.

She railed against wickedness and power.

Luke left us, to care for a sick man.

As we walked, Mother leaned on a stick. Her wrinkled face made me aware that the star of long ago was not around.

At Matthew's home we talked of John's betrayal.

Perhaps we should be somewhat mad to combat man's madness: we must chop up the two thousand crucifixes, chop them into pieces for firewood and with that firewood we shall bake our bread—our *pita*. Crucified bread is the bread of the poor, the waiting, waiting poor. God must help them; we must help them; we must help them as we must help God. Heal. Lift up our eyes.

Nazareth—home
Kislev 20

When I picked corn in a field with my disciples I was reproved because it was Sunday. When I healed the withered arm of a man I was rebuked because it was Sunday. I am threatened by various authorities for such "misdemeanors." Men spy on me and plot against me for acts of kindness. Kindness has reached the level of a crime. Officials remind me, rather discreetly, that John met a tragic death. The Sadducees hate me.

At the pool of Bethseda I helped a man who could not get into the water: I brought him health. He had been a paralytic for years. A cry went up because this was on a feast day. I explained that I intended to carry out my work regardless of the day.

"The son of man is lord even on the Sabbath," I said. "The world of kindness must be a part of our world."

At Nazareth, as I preached on a hill, the crowd turned on me. They insisted I perform miracles for them. Angered that I would not respond willy-nilly, men attempted to throw me off the cliffside of the hill. James, Mark and Phillip protected me; the four of us climbed down the cliff to a wadi.

Disgusted, Father feels I have gone out of my mind. He longs for the peace of my boyhood days. Mother understands: her feeling is intuitive. Though I disappoint and worry her she hides her concern, offering encouragement. She visits those I have healed and tells me how they have changed. Not all are like Simeon, grateful. Some do not want to have anything to do with me.

Peter's
Kislev 22

As I write Peter leans over my shoulder, reading this record that is such a poor record. In the midst of my writing I see John's face; I hear him. We talk about him.

"The Romans are going to take you, one of these days! What can I do to look after you? All of us...what can we do? Look at that madman the other day. He rushed at you... I thought he would kill you...he had a knife. And you cured his madness. There...there, he became one of us...or so it seems. Luke wants to help me look after you. You can't go on without any thought for yourself!"

Peter's voice expresses sincerity, warmth, education. Speech is man's finest quality. More than the eyes, the smile. Its powers are almost limitless. Its tenderness, the child, the babe. My mother consoles with a word perhaps. Out of the past it goes on and on with its revelations, its mirages.

Peter crumples leaves in his hands and reminisces as we sit around a table, the door open, his dog lying outside, flumping his tail agreeably.

"...No, Papa wasn't a clever fisherman. When Mama died he didn't look after our house; it didn't much matter to him what we had to eat. He seemed to be looking for her. I tried to light his lamp but it didn't work. He got very thin, weak; he coughed. I did all the fishing for us. I provided but I didn't do a very good job... I miss him...it was good to have him there, even when he was sick..."

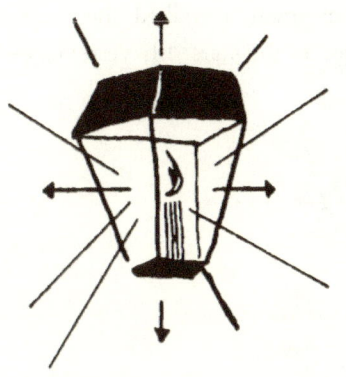

*I*n this little, comfortable house I try to find time in the evenings to study Greek or write in my journal. I prefer my journal. Doors wide open, the lamp bright, I read or write. My legs get restless, my eyes blink and the next thing I know the lamp has burned out and my room is dark.

The other night, after tossing on my pallet, I dreamed that a woman came and brought an antique alabaster box and knelt beside me—to anoint my feet. I tried to say something to her but I couldn't speak. The woman was beautiful.

Suddenly I was standing on a hill. A man was near me; there was nobody else. The man began repeating a parable, imitating me, each word curiously vivid. He said:

"There was a creditor who had two debtors. One owed his master five hundred but the other owed fifty." The speaker stopped, adjusted his purple robe. "When their master forgave them their debts who was the most grateful? The one who owed the most or the one who owed less?"

Someone laughed uproariously.

Ah, the strictures of the mind: without discipline we are weak. As a boy I learned values. I learned how to accept and how to refute. I remember holding a scroll against the light in the doorway of the synagogue: I noted how carefully each word was written. Pen strokes. Such a frail thing, this wisdom.

I found other kinds of wisdom on a dune, at a desert pool, in an oasis.

For days I have been trying to compose a meaningful prayer. I have trudged along the shore at Galilee; I have listened to the waves and gulls. I have tried to find words suitable for fisherfolk, villagers, countrymen. I walked the wadis, climbed the cliffs. I have lain in my tent and peered at the stars. I have repeated scriptures. Talked.

Last night, after supper, the words came to me:

> *Our Father Who art in heaven, hallowed be Thy name,*
> *Thy will be done,*
> *on earth as it is in heaven.*
> *Give us this day our daily bread, forgive us our trespasses,*
> *lead us not into temptation but deliver us from evil*
> *for Thine is the kingdom,*
> *the power and the glory, forever.*

When I repeated the prayer to Luke and Peter they were pleased.

Galilee
Tevet 11

A storm woke me as I lay in my tent. The wind was churning leaves and I walked to the lake to watch the waves. I felt cold but pulled my cloak around me and continued walking. Clouds were traveling fast. When the rain started I retraced my steps. I heard voices and men at their oars. Waves were piling against rocks. The voices in the boat sounded familiar. Again the thud of oars. Yells. Wasn't that Phillip? It was Peter. Through rain and spray I made out the hull of the boat; then I recalled someone saying they had to land a catch before dawn. Someone shouted:

"We're sinking...we're sinking!"

I walked over the water toward the boat; it was difficult to see through the rain and spray. I recognized the boat. As I walked the waves calmed; the water was black underfoot. Two of our men had slumped over their oars. I shouted. Nobody responded: they were frightened at seeing me. Peter cowered. I called again.

"Peter," I cried. " Don't you know me?"

"Is it you, Jesus?"

"Yes."

"Let me come to you."

"Come," I said.

He sank as he walked toward me and I caught his arm and steadied him and helped him climb into his boat. Luke welcomed me. The boat swung toward me and I got in and sat at the stern with Phillip. Everyone began bailing. The rain was letting up and I pointed to the shore. We soon beached her and everyone began to talk, telling his panic, that they had been unable to see; they crowded around me; they thought I had saved their lives.

Luke built a fire of beachwood and as the sun came up we had breakfast together—some of them singing, everyone hungry, the fish tasting marvelous.

"Mark broke his oar," Luke said and laughed. He was drying by the fire, his clothes steaming. He explained that they had been blown first one way and then another.

Nain
Tevet 18

This has been a beautiful week because I raised a man from the dead and made a blind man see.

At Nain, a small village, my disciples and I met a burial procession headed for tombs cut in the side of a nearby hill. A young man lay on a flower-covered bier. I learned his name from a man in the procession: it was David. He and his mother had been my friends for years. I recognized Athalia walking behind the bier, weeping. Aaron, her husband, had died recently.

It was a warm, still afternoon. The warbling of a bulbul seemed out of place as the procession passed. As the bier scraped against a rock, as the bearers stopped, I approached one of them and asked them to wait.

"David...David...this is Jesus...arise..."

The disciples, astonished, bunched around the bier. I touched David, spoke loudly, shook him.

"David, you are all right. Your mother is here. Get up..." He sat up among his flowers and his mother rushed to his side. He recognized my voice and asked for me. I talked gently with him.

A happy procession. The bier was abandoned; someone threw flowers into the air as David walked...

I am overjoyed as I write. I see David and his mother kissing each other. Someone is singing.

From Nain I went on to see the daughter of Jairus as she lay in bed in her home. The curtains were drawn; the air was sick room air; flowers had wilted on her bed table; her dog cringed under her bed. I asked everyone to leave us alone.

"*Talitha cumi*," I said. "Daughter, I say arise...you are no longer ill. The fever has left you." As I prayed I also thought of John and his death. This little girl was not to fill a grave. I bent over her and took her hand. I could see her rolling a hoop, laughing.

"*Talitha cumi*," I repeated, and sat beside her, pressed my hand over her forehead, touched her eyelids. "Rise, my daughter...you must sleep no longer..."

Her eyes flashed; she was afraid because she had never seen me; smiling, I said:

"Your mother is outside your room...shall I call her?" She nodded.

When I came to the blind man in his home I pressed my fingers over his eyes and spoke to him. I wet clay and placed it over his eyes. I allowed the cool clay to comfort him as I spoke; his wife watched with an expression of doubt; as I removed the clay she stepped aside.

He made a curious noise, pushed me aside, stood.

Walking, he asked:

"Is this my home...is that my garden out there? Are you the man called Jesus of Nazareth? That must be a tree out there..." He was walking into the garden of his home. "Is that...is that a bird...who are the people watching me...and that, is that a flower?"

I write and the evening sun shines on my table and on my hands and it seems to me that I have lived many years in a short span; it seems to me I am very much alone; it seems to me I hear voices: Deuteronomy voices, Jeremiah voices. I hear and yet I am alone. Today is my birthday. I am thirty-three.

s a boy I respected Greek—such a rich vocabulary, I found; I thought the language overly concise. Hebrew is the city man's tongue, best suited to argument. I prefer my Aramaic. It is more gracious and agreeable for public speaking.

Haran believed in learning three languages: he was the most intelligent rabbi I have met. To him I owe my background; his years of tutoring gave me freedom to think. Morning after morning we sat facing each other at his home.

"We have to think, not memorize...you memorize and then force memories to evolve into patterns of original thought. Yes, memory and thought are brothers. But, make no mistake, thousands repeat the law and the scriptures and only a handful think."

I see his sparsely bearded, wan face. He was a man who ate sparingly yet lived to be eighty. A great walker, he was as restless in body as in mind.

Haran was proud of two ancient scrolls—one of them on copper. The library at Qumran had greater rarities of course.

Haran said:

"Something lives in you...your mother has called my attention to it, an inner voice. When I heard you declaim in the synagogue I perceived it."

So, it is my privilege to help, merge dream and fulfillment: I believe it is a privilege no other man has had: I am the husbandman.

> *Come unto me ye who labor and are heavy laden and I will give you rest...suffer the little children to come...*

Tonight I see the world shining in their eyes; I hear hope in their prattle.

Years ago I experienced the greatness of the Sinai desert, its crags and dunes, the heat and cold. I came to understand its desolation, its loneliness, its calm and fury. Now, during these troubled times, I long to return to the Sinai...have a lizard sit beside me, my straw-covered basket filled with golden dates.

In the Sinai I perfected my Greek to a greater extent and studied the classical

Hebrew until it came easily. The history of man became an important part of my meditations. Silence and the simoom became part of those devotions.

A tiny plant sprouted outside my tent and withstood the heat, cold and winds. It was my companion and incentive, a little calendar in leaves.

I found the same plant growing at Qumran, behind the monastery. While I studied there it survived several sand storms.

Locusts, dates, bread, honey—the wilderness taught me the true taste of food. During the months since the wilderness I have eaten well, too well, but the taste is lacking.

I have not thought as clearly as I thought when unencumbered by men. There, each morning was mine, each evening was mine. Worship was as natural as breathing.

My tent flaps billowed. They were pinned back every night by the stars. Heat and thirst were often there yet a sense of praise was foremost. Wonderment was on top of a dune. As I slept a mirage might come and bathe me in its cool water.

I slept on my boyhood blanket, one woven by my mother. She wove it when I was ten.

Nazareth
Shevat 15

I am leaving Nazareth—leaving home.

It is farewell to friends and places, all I have loved. Only in memory will I walk along the orchard creek and hunt for crayfish, think and stare as a boy thinks and stares. I had several pals... We had niches in cliffs where we often hid. We had an old fig we liked to climb; there was a cave where we lit fires. We found menhirs and dolmen—strange, strange things! In Galilee we had a stout little boat and we'd drift, drop anchor, fish for chromis and watch the pelicans.

There's a feeling to my Nazareth: the stars are brighter there, the sun seems a little bigger, the wind a little cooler. How good it was to turn a corner and think: Mama's home...supper is almost ready...Papa's working in his shop.

Today was cool and windy.

I visited Simeon. I visited Mark. I visited Jude. I called on the captain, who has been transferred to Nazareth. His son sat in my lap a while. I did not say good-bye although I lingered at each place. I wanted to feel the peace of each place and keep it with me. I did not need to talk much. Being with friends was all I asked.

Oh, how the wind blew me along, flapping my cloak, flapping the olive branches, the weeds and the papyrus.

How hard it is to write.

Nazareth

Before I left home Father displayed the gifts of the Magi on his work bench, first removing his tools and shavings. He locked the door and lit two candles. Mother—so excited—seemed to be seeing the star as she handled the gifts.

"They haven't changed... Joseph, you've taken good care of them! Oh, they're so beautiful!"

And she knelt in the sawdust, the gold cup in her hands, its jewels redder than I had remembered. I had forgotten the gifts were so beautiful.

"Where have you kept them...in the synagogue? The geniza?" I asked.

Father nodded, frowning.

"We have decided to present them to the elders...tomorrow...at the meeting. They'll become the temple possessions. It's different with you going away... Mother and I have decided..."

But I wasn't listening; I was absorbed in Mother's appreciation as she handled the gifts, kneeling or half-kneeling, smiling; her shoulders lost some of their age. The myrrh box interested me, its aroma still evident, its chased lid yet untarnished. Mother lifted the clasp. The clasp was set with green stones. She called my attention to the ornamented hinges. She held out the gold cup to my father...

"I wish you hadn't worried about the gifts," she said with a sigh. "We ought to have enjoyed them...now we can see them at the temple... Look, Jesus, at this handle...ah, those were strange days in Bethlehem... God was with us..."

I loved her for her dreams and sacrifices.

I loved the hints of youth and beauty in her face.

Nazareth
Shevat 25

Tomorrow is my last day here.

As I lay on my pallet I heard rain lash our roof; I heard the wind in the trees. Then my mind dropped back and I remembered Mother singing, crooning to me, as I lay sick as a boy. I remembered songs in the evening. I heard her laughter as we played jacks. I smelled her barley bread... I smelled roasting lamb... Father was in his workshop, his plane sliding; he was singing. As a child I loved his singing.

Now, silent, worried, he works in a preoccupied state, bothered by frequent visitors, concerned about my future. "It is wrong of you to go to Jerusalem, wrong to throw yourself into the hands of your enemies."

There will be no more Festivals of Light.

At Nazareth I used to have a pet goat.

Memories... I can not tolerate juvenile memories any longer. I am not an old man. Memories must not impede my ministry.

There must be beauty. Life must have beauty.

Jerusalem
Shevat 29

Thy rod and Thy staff will comfort me...yeah, though I walk through the valley of death yet will I be with Thee.

As I walked into Jerusalem I heard those words. It was dusk. An immense caravan choked the air, camels, drivers, gapers. Again I thought of Herod and the innocents: city life brings Herod to mind. The *Kittim* are evident on the main streets: helmets, standards, shields.

A camel sank to the ground beside me, eying me, begging for kindness. Trumpets blared.

Crowds circled the temple, some chanting, some bearing fruit, some waving palm fronds. Flares burned. On two giant candelabra, perhaps eighty feet high, torches smoked, guttered.

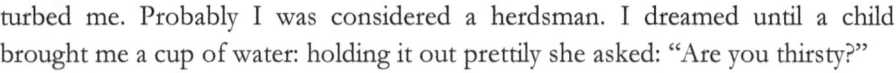

Shall I be able to help the people of Jerusalem? Shall I remain? My loneliness here was so unlike the loneliness of the desert.

I was to meet Judas who was to take me to friends. When he did not come I bedded down in a booth of branches, with cattle nearby.

I slept and woke to their animal sounds, without dread. Someone roused the oxen, then the sheep; the beasts wanted to be fed and watered. Nobody disturbed me. Probably I was considered a herdsman. I dreamed until a child brought me a cup of water: holding it out prettily she asked: "Are you thirsty?"

"Yes," I said.

"My papa is taking care of the oxen."

Opening my pouch I offered sugared dates to the girl.

I found Judas at the home of a mutual friend. I had never seen him so well dressed. He drew me aside and gave me money from our treasury. He seemed forlorn. I am told he is having a love affair with the daughter of Pilate. Marcus, the son of a senator, has described Pilate's daughter as a beautiful, talented, ruthless woman. Marcus and I sat on a garden bench and he enthused about Jerusalem: "So unlike Rome, so much more oriental—can it be we are free of our penates here?"

That evening I stayed in the house of Leonidas Clibus. My windows were olive tree windows. Garden paths circled a tiny fountain where someone had tossed fresh oleander blossoms, red blossoms.

A copy of Horace lay on a circular table by my bed; lamps and rugs, hangings

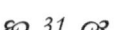

and x-shaped Roman chairs, cushions and inlaid boxes brightened the room. Propped on a cushion I read Horace for hours; when my candles dimmed a slave brought me fresh candles and volumes by Lucretius—recent translations.

> *...What's this wanton lust for life*
> *To make us tremble in dangers and in doubt?*
> *All men must die and no man can escape.*
> *We turn and turn in the same atmosphere...*

I went to sleep preferring the thoughts of Horace: his love of nature, his fondness for rustic surroundings, his boating on the river Aufidus, his fishing. He liked to play ball. I could visualize him, as a boy, when wood pigeons covered him with leaves as he slept on a hillside.

*T*here are children here. What priceless looks they give. I love their delight in simple things, their warmth, their trust, so obvious, so quick. Truly, theirs is a special kingdom. I am happiest when they are around me, as they were yesterday in Clibus' garden. It was a birthday party for his daughter who is six. I told stories as they sat around me. What laughter, giggles. A little boy brought me a toad and put it in my hand, saying:

"It's for you, Atta."

Clibus

Of course I miss the great library at Qumran. The beautiful library in his home is a fraction of that monastic collection but bearded Clibus has invited me—with widespread arms.

A delicate bronze of Minerva stands on a plinth at the window end of the narrow room.

A book on my lap, I watched a golden Persian cat steal about, stiffly independent.

Though I can not read Latin I can understand titles and the names of authors and I appreciate handsome volumes, ancient volumes, family treasures.

Minerva—I used to think of visiting Rome and Athens.

Adar 15

I spoke to a group near the city gate. I was aware that officials were present, Sadducees.

I saw men dragging a woman, kicking her, letting her fall. She had been caught in adultery. When she was brought to me I suspected a trick. Why should I pass judgment when officials were in the crowd? Authorities wanted me to break the law by passing judgment.

I was shocked by the woman's fear, her beseeching face. As she stood by me a soldier hit her with a chain. Men yelled: "Stone her, stone her!" When a man shoved her to her knees she hid her face in her arms—pretty, a country girl, I thought.

To give myself time to think I wrote on the ground with a stick. I wrote and obliterated words, watching the crowd and the woman. I smelled death. It was in the smoke of sacrifices burning in the city. It was in the crowd around me. I had never smelled the death of a person.

Taking in the street ruffians and the officials I said, in a loud voice:

"Look at her, at her torn clothes. Do any of you know her? Think. Go deep inside. Think. Let the man who has not sinned throw the first stone. You accuse her...where is the man? Go home, all of you. Have you no pity? Remember the commandment: Thou shalt not kill. We are not animals! Let her go... I repeat, let her go. Go home—all of you!"

I helped the woman to stand. Someone had thrown ashes on her face and I bought water at a shop and washed her face and hands and bought oil for her cuts and bruises. Matthew found us and brought her food.

"Where can I hide?" she asked us. "What is to become of me? They will catch me...beat me... Master, master...what shall I do?" Her words mixed with sobs.

Matthew and I helped her out of town, beyond the gates. We sent her to the home of Talus where Luke cares for the sick.

I returned to Clibus' library but I was too disturbed to read. While I sat there, the *Sayings of Moses* spread before me, Affti, Clibus' Egyptian wife, brought a pillow and sat by me. She is as beautiful as Miriam; to have her there was a comfort but her words were not comforting:

"It isn't safe for you to preach in Jerusalem... Your faith is for the little towns and villages where the Romans have less influence or none at all...

"When James was here a month or so ago he mentioned going to Rome. Do you wish him to preach your gospel there?"

She went on to urge me to send apostles to Egypt.

"There are more than seventy of you now... I hope you can send two or more to my country...to preach in the villages...you are needed there."

That evening, after dinner, she rapped on my door: she is very tall, very elegant; dressed in an Egyptian gown, she made a little bow, and presented me with a bronze stylus.

"It will be better than your wooden one," she said.

While enjoying my stylus someone brought me a dish of lemon paste.

Sadly, more than twenty years have passed since our Nazareth synagogue acquired a scroll. Our scrolls are in tatters and all are asked to refrain from using them. Learning this, Clibus has offered several scrolls.

"I'll send two of my men...one to carry the scrolls, the other to see that the first man doesn't wander off."

Perhaps little Nazareth may have a worthwhile collection someday.

Jerusalem
Adar 20

My enemies come closer.

> *Verily, I say unto you, the man who climbs the sheepfold wall is a thief.*
> *He who enters by the gate is the shepherd. To him the porter opens and the*
> *sheep hear his voice and he calls his sheep by name and leads them...*

My parable is realistic but people do not listen. They push one another, talk.

When I encountered a blind man, a man who had never seen during his lifetime, I sent him to the Siloam pool. He bathed there and at my touch his sight became normal. He stumbled, fell, rushed about, shouted. Trembling he raced for home. He brought friends and there was great rejoicing. Then, stunning everyone, authorities questioned me rudely. Because he defended me and called me his healer he was put in jail.

I had to go before the local magistrate, affirm his honesty; then he was freed. I said to the magistrate:

"I came into this world to help men see..."

Last week I cured lepers on the Jericho road, men and women, all in rags. All were afraid of me, afraid of themselves. I thought I could change their minds but their minds were in tatters like their clothes. One man thanked me, a young man from Tyre; the others, quarrelling, pushing one another, tearing at their rags, left the road to crawl into a cave.

I asked the man from Tyre what he knew about the others but he could not concentrate on what I said: he was so moved, so pleased, so enraptured over his health he stood in front of me, smiling, laughing. He kept holding up his arms and hands—showing me. I asked him about people I knew in Tyre. He shook his head, laughed, kissed my hands, rushed off. A caravan was passing, camels, drivers, onlookers; he disappeared among the camels, the dust.

Jerusalem
Adar 25

Today I received a message: the *mebakker* at Qumran has invited me to return to the monastery for a second residency. He wants me to instruct others in the Messianic Rule.

I am no longer in accord with Qumran's rigid communal life: such sharing would be difficult for me; certainly none of my disciples would understand.

But I think of the Qumran desert; I think of the cliffs and caves near the monastery. Morning and evening shadows! What great fogs used to engulf us!

Urusalim
Adar 28

I spoke outside the temple and, as I spoke, men and boys picked up stones to throw at me.

Sadducees want me excluded from the temple; others want me excommunicated. They stamp me an untouchable. Such intrigue! How am I to help mankind? My disciples urge me to leave Jerusalem. The world is beautiful, they remind me: Go to Cana, go to Bethlehem, to Galilee, to Jericho. Date groves. Olive groves. Roses. As if I needed a reminder.

This afternoon I walked about Solomon's city to an impressive ruin, a series of roofless rooms, fallen columns, weeds growing through marble floors, lizards on walls. Birds dotted the sky. I tried to imagine the regal furnishings of Ptolemy's time. Underfoot were hieroglyphic slabs, a cartouche among them. I climbed old stone walls, were they Nehemiah's walls when he fortified the city? I found a broken scarab and remembered Egyptian words my mother taught me as a boy. In the street below the vast ruins a Roman soldier talked with another Roman soldier. Herod's workmen were capping stone pillars. Tall men in dark red robes, red turbans on their heads, prodded camels, heavily laden animals. Were they Syrians?

Somewhere along the way I met a blind man led by a boy. The sun sent sweat down the boy's face. Tired, they sat by a spring where women and girls were filling jars. People recognized me and soon a crowd formed, as I rested. The blind man, wearing a sash woven with gold, white-bearded, tall, erect and proud, asked about me. The boy whispered desperately to him.

"It's Bartimaeus and his son, from Jericho," a woman said.

"Son of David, have mercy on me," Bartimaeus pled, speaking softly. Then he cried:

"Lord, have mercy, that I may receive my sight. Are you Jesus of Nazareth? Will you help me? Will you touch my eyes? I must see again."

I sat close to him and talked to him, the aura of his faith evident. As we talked I realized he could see: his expressions were so startling. He embraced his son. Erect, silent, he stared about him. Everyone was silent. Fumbling a little, he walked away; then, he returned and knelt by me and kissed my hands.

"Master...let me follow you... I believe...let me be one of your chosen...let me tell others what you have done for me. I know about your ministry." He kissed my robe. "When I heard you speak yesterday I tried to reach you."

He urged me to stay at his home; perhaps he had heard me say that fox have holes and birds have nests but the man of God has no home. I warned Bartimaeus not to look back if he put his hand to the plough.

Lately I have not seen much of Judas. He refuses to visit me at Clibus' home. I hear that Judas has quarrelled with the daughter of Pilate. Faithful to our group, he collects and disperses funds. Our group is increasing in number—committed to everyone. Some of us provide food, clothing and shelter.

A nomad group is famine stricken. The babies need sugar and salt and we have provided packets by way of a caravan.

Clibus'

Through Clibus I have written a letter home. Mother will find someone to read it aloud. I don't want Mother and Father to come here. They dislike the city. Father has been unable to work and needs to husband his strength. He must avoid danger.

Getting up at dawn I have been able to memorize lines from Horace, lines that help. The tiny garden helps. The children help. But when John's cousin, Elihu, came, distortion returned as we talked of John's imprisonment, torture, death. Elihu is a frail soul, so unlike John. He is so in need of encouragement. He tells me that a storm flooded homes in Nazareth. They did the best they could with shovels and baskets.

I look forward to resurrection. The promise of resurrection sustains me although I am, at times, confused, confused because resurrection means a blurring of the future, perhaps a cessation of the future. I can not plan a sabbath. I can not say "We shall meet together at Samaria." Since the beyond is truly incomprehensible today is distorted as well.

I must warn myself of the onslaught of pain that will crush me during the crucifixion. How to bear it? Gird my loins, perhaps. It will not be easy to die for my fellowmen. Will my ascension help others rise from their tragic lives?

Dread eats away at me.

Hate undermines me.

Broken covenants...Golgotha, place of skulls...rocky Judea... Caesar Augustus, your crimes are everywhere...imperator...killer!

I need to be baptized with love.

With wisdom.

Yesterday, in this city of rocks, I noticed straw in a stable, yellow straw, fresh, clean, glistening in the sun. I took a few. Straw is simplicity. Simplicity points to a balanced way.

Yesterday I walked to Bethany. Martha and Mary said that Lazarus had died. Among graves and stunted trees, in a stinging wind, I became keenly aware of the days I spent at their home, with the three of them. How often Lazarus and I had done carpentering under his thatched shed.

Here, with his sisters, friends and relatives, here at the tombs, I knew death was not the answer. I walked to the crypt where Lazarus lay. Loose rocks tumbled underfoot. Wind whipped. A boulder blocked the crypt and I asked Martha to have her friends help me drag it aside. Men consulted and argued that it was useless; they glared at me savagely as they pushed and dragged the stone.

At the opening I bent over and cried:

"Lazarus...come... I am the resurrection and the life...come...this is Jesus!"

I needed him. His family needed him. Mary and Martha. Death did not need him, surely.

Men jeered and howled. But I knelt and shouted as the wind spat on all of us.

Ah, sorrowing women, yellow rocks, death, a man in his crypt, cold stone, a hawk screaming...

I called again and again.

"Lazarus, this is Jesus. Arise! Come with us! Remember us, remember I am the resurrection and the life. Come unto me...believe...God is here..."

It was late afternoon: the sun was behind the yellow cliff.

Martha clutched my arm and said:

"Lord, let us leave. Lazarus has been dead four days. He stinks."

A funeral procession passed by—men and women—the men carrying a child's coffin.

"God, our Father, help us. Give this man life again!" I beseeched with passion. I knew, as I prayed, that Lazarus would respond.

Swaying, wrapped in burial clothes, Lazarus appeared, a scarf across his face. He could not see or move his hands. I went to him and Martha uncovered his eyes. Mary ran to help. We unwrapped his legs and arms.

"Jesus has given you life," Martha said. "You are going home with us...you are one of us again."

Stumbling over rocks, Mary guiding him, Lazarus found a place to sit down. We unbound him and someone gave him a robe. Someone offered him a piece of bread. He shook his head, stared at us, turned from one to the other, his face birdlike, hawklike, white. He peered at his crypt. Martha hugged him, laughing. People gathered. Some knelt around us.

"Mary, what happened?" Lazarus began, speaking his first words.

"Why am I here in this place? Why am I wearing a robe? And these people... and Jesus! Was I sick? Where are my clothes?"

I longed to leave this place of death: it was closing in on me. The wind blew harder and a hawk leaped upward.

With Martha I walked away, listening to her happiness, her praise.

"We must have supper. What shall we eat? Will he be hungry, able to eat? Jesus, you have saved him. I love you. It's wonderful! He's back...think of it, after four days. Then, then there is no death for us who believe..."

At supper Lazarus was unable to talk; he drank a little and soon had bread wet with olive oil. No one had much to say. Lazarus sat next to me. Bending over his plate he gave me a few boyish grins—like old times. He had gotten into his work clothes. Putting his hand into a pocket he pulled out a small chisel and laid it on the table. But he said nothing. I urged him to eat Martha's fish or lamb, delicately prepared. Every face at the table expressed a wonderment and rapture. The candles burned down. The women ate. Suddenly there was chatter and then laughter—rejoicing.

It was difficult to return to Jerusalem, leave my friends. I lingered a day for the fields of barley, the paths that were peaceful paths. I had to have time to be with Lazarus, be with Mary and Martha, write my journal. Alongside the carpentry bench I have a table. I prefer writing outdoors. There is a vine on the thatched shed and it is in flower. As I write Lazarus is sleeping on the ground, in the sun.

Caretakers at the graveyard claim that one of the crypts has been robbed.

Jerusalem

I keep hearing the words of an old hymn as I go about; it was John's favorite, one we learned while at Qumran. Was it solace while he was imprisoned? I hope it was. It is a comfort to me—so gracious.

> *I give thanks unto Thee, O Lord,*
> *For Thou has wrought a wonder with dust.*
> *Thou hast made me know Thy deep, deep truth,*
> *Thou hast given me a voice;*
> *I continually bless Thy name.*

I seem to hear John's commanding voice, his loving benediction as I left his prison:

> *The Lord bless thee and keep thee,*
> *the Lord make His face to shine upon thee*
> *and be gracious unto thee...*

Ephraim
Nisan 14

I am staying at a beautiful old stone house in nearby Ephraim. I have allowed myself a respite, among pomegranate, olives, roses. Herons fly at dawn and evening. Children run in and out. A boy with shaggy head has a pet dove. A girl with almond eyes is learning to weave. My disciples are here, the new and the old. We have met in a low room, plain and bearded men, clothes new and disheveled; Ezra shows me his injured leg; Luke works over it; Lamech (a strong youth) is from Casarea, an expert swimmer, he said.

"I will walk to Jerusalem tomorrow. I'll remain there. The high priests will accost me. They may mock and scourge me, as they have many others...but I will return." I tried to speak calmly. I could not be forthright...

Calling me "Rabboni," a pretty girl knelt in the jammed room and anointed me with fragrant oil. It was a moment of calm, a moment of beauty.

Nisan 15

Holy Week has begun.

I walk accompanied by my disciples.

As we pass a tall wooden cross I remembered that the Romans have crucified as many as two thousand men at one time because of religious dedication. Almost every single one of us has witnessed a crucifixion.

Hail Caesar!

Ours was a solemn path on a clear morning, larks singing, the air brisk.

Carrying fronds, waving, hoping to speak to us, hundreds filled the paths and streets, wanting the miracle of love and life.

Our path crooked upward to the "House of the Figs," where I was given a donkey, a tall, white one. Children shouted joyously. For me, he was my donkey of peace. I waved as I rode along. Some women cut branches and tossed them in front of me. Others threw flowers and shouted "Hosanna."

Jerusalem spread around me, blocks of stone, yellow walls, piles of ancient masonry, new porticos, towers, shops... It was my city, my hated city; I esteemed the meaning it has for my forefathers, men who slept in the valley, with peaked cypresses above their graves.

Dust fanned over us as we followed a narrow way. Romans turned on me and turned on the crowd but I warned them to desist.

At the temple I found more money changers. The courtyard was cattleyard; waiting rooms were storerooms. Animals bellowed. I struck again at the vendors, toppling tables, hurling money trays. The crowd screamed, cheered. In the midst of this bedlam strangers, travelers, stopped Philip and Andrew. They insisted upon being presented to me. The four men offered me sanctuary in the kingdom of Edessa.

Priests, soldiers, young and old crammed around me as I explained the life eternal, the image of redemption, eternal salvation and the price we must pay.

God is our Father...the world of nature proclaims His goodness...men must share His divine harmony...you reach God from within...reborn, you recognize the light.

Children sang.

My love went to them.

Astride my donkey I preached to them in simple words.

As the sun slipped behind the city towers there were scores listening and we lingered on the terrace:

"There is light for you for a little while longer...walk while there is light... darkness will come...he who walks in darkness cannot tell where he is going... believe in the light..."

The evening air was becoming chilly; a wind was blowing in from the desert.

With my twelve I walked through the Golden Gate, passing great herds of sheep and goats, grey pastoral sheep and black mountain goats. I was proud of my men, proud of their courage and love, proud of their humility.

Jerusalem
Nisan 29

We met in an upper room—a white-walled room. Centering it was a long table and we sat around it, sharing bread and wine...below us roses were in flower.

God was with me as I told them, my legatees, that I must die.

"Tonight you are entrusted with the keys of the kingdom. Two at a time you are to go about the world, preaching the gospel. Faith is our church."

I loved each man. Such faces! Bartholomew, Matthew, Luke, James, Simon, Peter, Thaddeus, Judas, John, Phillip. I gazed at one and then the other, fisherman, cobbler, farmer, physician, lawyer...brothers.

"Your task is to save mankind!"

The lamps on our table shaped shadows on the walls, on the floor, far more than shadows. The white walls enshrined each of us. When the wind puffed our lamps blinked. Ours was an aura that may never recur.

"Soon my enemies will crucify me...one of you will betray me..."

What consternation! What hysterical exclamations! What accusations! Then the pleas began: you must escape! Let us help you! We can! Listen...flee...tonight.

"Faith is the miracle for everyone," I said. "Heal the sick. Remember Cana... Galilee...Lazarus...the lepers on the roadway..."

I reminded them that we are samaritans. Mercy is ours, ours to give. We are to help the heavy laden. Love our children. We are to teach by example.

Israel, I told myself, you are to nurture goodwill, tolerance, peace, hope.

So it was in that white room, at that hour.

Clibus'

By the light of candles I write, to shepherd words, to commune once more. There is little time for writing, little time for thinking. I feel that I must endure. By the flickering lights I commune with Father, Mother, earth.

I would like to go on healing the sick, alleviating pain, the body's pain, the soul's. To be a good shepherd, yes. Will my disciples persevere?

I can write no more tonight.

O h, Jerusalem, you killer of prophets, stoner of those sent to help you! How I have wanted to care for your children as a hen cares for her chicks under her wings. You would not have me!

Plotters have attempted to trap me. A group cornered me near the temple. Is it lawful to pay tribute to Caesar? they asked. I asked for a coin. I called their attention to the face on the coin, the face of Caesar Augustus.

"Render to Caesar the things that are Caesar's and unto God the things that are God's."

Not to be defeated, men queried me, as I sat in the court of the temple, old, old questions. It seemed to me they were stunned when I reminded them that God is not the god of the dead but of the living. Other interrogators appeared at noon. A huge grey-bearded priest demanded:

"Master, which is the greatest commandment of the law?"

I deliberated, wanting to impose on his arrogance.

"You shall love the Lord will all your heart and with your soul and with your mind...this is the first and greatest commandment," I said. "The second commandment is similar," I pointed out. "You shall love your neighbor as yourself."

By now I was angry and left these idlers and when I was alone with my disciples I shamed the trouble-makers who clean the outside of the cup and leave the inside dirty... I called them a generation of vipers...they are the ones who will persecute the faithful from town to town...crucify them...

Grief overcame me. I could talk no longer.

Disgusted with the day, Matthew asked if the world would come to an end soon. That question had to be left unanswered. Inventors of questions are everywhere. I wanted to add, watch, be on guard, pray ceaselessly, work... Don't be careless while your master is away. You can't tell when he may return.

Mother came to visit me, she arrived in the night, afraid. Rumors had reached her that I was ill. She was ill. It is a long, long walk, from Nazareth. Peter gave us melon and though it was long past midnight we sat at a little table under the stars and ate.

It is impossible to go on writing.

I see what is to take place. I am frightened. I must wait until I have risen from the dead to continue writing. I have spoken to Matthew. I will entrust my journal to him.

Judas, in a drunken rage, has gone to the authorities and has promised to deliver me to them for a sum. He ridiculed me when I refused to ask God's protection.

Here are my final thoughts:

I beg You, dear Lord, hear me. Be attentive to my last supplications.

I wait, my soul waits. My soul waits for You more than any who wait for the morning. I say, more than those who watch for the morning.

Peter's
Iyyar 10

I am alive.

A tremor roused me and I slowly unwound my grave clothes, noticing how beautiful they were. I looked at my left hand. I looked at my right hand. They had healed. The stone that blocked my crypt had been rolled aside. It was dawn when I went out. Outside I found a discarded robe.

The sky was grey but sun slanted across spring hills. I walked toward the sun on a path that led away from the tombs. Perhaps no one can grasp my bewilderment and my happiness. I tasted the air. My brain rushed about, rebounded from a bush, crashed against rocks. Light was splintering around me; inside that light was the realization that my suffering is over. I need not die. Life was living in me like a seed, but a perpetual seed.

Following a path across flowering fields I picked flowers; then, across the field, I saw Mary Magdalene. She was sobbing, crying. I called her and she ran to me, saying "Rabboni" over and over. "Dearest..."

Mary and Martha appeared. The women surrounded me, laughing, touching me, kissing my robe, my hands. Later in the day we set out for Nazareth, for my home, Mother and Father. Halfway Mother met us and threw her arms around me—no words were necessary.

That evening, as we ate together, Mother described Father's imprisonment. He had sold the gifts of the Magi to obtain bribe money: he planned to bribe the soldiers to free me. The merchant who bought the gifts summoned officials. By lying he got Father jailed for theft.

It required four days to free him, our Nazarene priests testifying...

Liberated from death I see life as a singular continuity, a continuity embodying my imperfections, many hopes. I find a new calm in all that I experience: as I project into tomorrow I sense this serenity. Simplicity itself wears an aura of riches.

Tonight, living in this composure, I write freely. Time, as a force, has dropped away. Pressures are comprehensible such as the stress at our last supper, the betrayal of Judas. Though I held my emotions in check I felt confused by many doubts: above all I felt that my ministry would fail. Ah, that white room, those shadows, our courage as we sipped salt water in memory of the Egyptian exodus. Those faces as we sang. Now those memories are glassed inside a mirror, unblemished. And I may open that mirror and experience a memory or I may close the surface.

I stand alone. It is a beautiful feeling. I stand here without past and without future. I am a naked man, a man of the wilderness. This is the miracle of self.

The mind owns itself. It does not ask. Acceptance blocks out intrusion. Each of us should experience the wilderness of mind.

Iyyar 18

This is how it was:

As I knelt in the garden I thought of John and his prison bars, for around me were bars of shrubbery, blacker than any I had seen. Immobile bars.

Death was in the bars and in the air around me, imagined but none the less real, as real as death had been in the street that day men wanted to stone the woman taken in adultery. This was my death—I listened for approaching soldiers, for the voice of Judas.

"If it is possible," I prayed, "let this cup pass from me quickly."

I heard the brook below: it had a place to go. I had this, this waiting, this expectancy, my disciples asleep on the ground.

Death...death is the ransom for man's sin, I reminded myself.

Cries of sentinels rang out.

Judas knew that I was here, that I had come here to pray; presently I heard the unmistakable clank of side arms and men's voices, foreign speech. I could wait no longer. I stood up and waited for Judas to identify me.

Stumbling over shrubbery, Judas called.

I answered.

"Who are you looking for?" I asked a soldier carrying a torch.

"Jesus of Nazareth," he said.

"I am Jesus."

Lanterns and torches appeared. Peter saw and heard the soldiers and snatching a sword from one of the guards he slashed a man's ear. I rebuked him and cared for the guard, an Arabian named Malchus, who was singularly afraid of me, afraid of the garden, his task.

"We shouldn't have come...you were praying...this is the garden where you come to pray," Malchus said.

"Is Judas with you?" I asked.

"He has gone... I'm captain here...you must come with us. We have been commanded to take you to the high priest, Ananias."

"You take me with swords and shields—like a thief. I taught in the temple... I prayed daily for you..."

Malchus, his face in torchlight, mumbled in Arabian and turned away.

"Leave him alone...get out of here," Peter shouted; I saw the guards struggle with him.

Malchus led me along the narrow streets, dark. People lay asleep in corners and doorways. Donkeys were hobbled together. We walked over piles of garbage. As we filed toward the house of Ananias wind smoked our torches. At the door of the house we were kept waiting. Two of my guards fell asleep.

Amid bickering I was led into a small room and left there; then, late in the morning, I was brought before Caiaphas, before scribes and elders, in an open courtyard. There I heard someone say that it is expedient for us that he die for his people.

Caiaphas asked me about my teachings and I responded:

"I have spoken openly. I have taught in the synagogues of Nazareth and Cana and Capernaum and in this city... I have said nothing in secret. Ask those who have heard me what I have said." I spoke tersely because I realized this was a false trial.

One of the scribes struck me across my face and hurled me to the floor.

Witnesses were brought—citizens. One testified that I had vowed to destroy the temple within three days and rebuild it without hands. Other witnesses disagreed. A woman said I faked miracles. A man testified I had threatened to depose the governor. Others disagreed.

"Are you Christ...are you the man the people call Christ?" Caiaphas asked.

"I am."

A priest gestured; he seemed to tear his robe. Caiaphas smiled.

"You have heard this blasphemy," he said. "We need no more witnesses. I condemn this man to death." I knew nothing more could be said in my defense.

As I sit at my table, underneath the trees, at Peter's home, I write as if I were writing about someone else, a friend perhaps. I write without prejudice. I am shaken by man's corruption and yet my lack of faith in man does not influence my writing.

I was left in the hands of guards and palace servants and then I was led into a room where my hands were roped behind me. I was thrown on the floor and beaten and kicked and spat on. Men placed me in a chair and covered my eyes and asked me to guess who struck me, everyone laughing.

I fell asleep on the floor and was wakened for a trial before priests, elders, scribes, in a marble-floored room, Roman insignia on the wall, the room icy, airless, officers and soldiers at one end, one of them in battle gear—to impress me, I thought. But I was scarcely able to stand, scarcely able to think. My hands on the back of a chair, I put my mind to work: I singled out my home, its doors, its windows, the grass growing in the street. I forced myself to visualize my mother and father. Though I was in pain I remembered my little friend, Amos: we were kneeling in the dust before my house, playing marbles: dust flipped as we shot.

I was asked if I was the son of God.

The trial was not a trial. There were no witnesses.

Temple officials conferred.

Roman authority was not involved.

A judge or priest condemned me to death.

Such authority had been denied forty years ago by the Romans. Being aware of this added to my resentment; I tried to speak out but was silenced. From the courtyard I was marched to the paved square called Babbatha; troops lined the square, spectators gathered. The sun's warmth lessened my pain. One of the guards, secretly, gave me bread. I saw Judas with Pontius Pilate; Pilate was accompanied by councilors, guards. I felt I had been hurled into a wholly alien world—enemy world.

Pilate, stepping forward in his robe, asked Caiaphas the nature of my crime. I will remember that scarlet robe.

Caiaphas, annoyed, said:

"If he were not a malefactor we would not bring him before you." Pilate understood the evasion. He responded:

"Take him, judge him according to your law."

A priest declared:

"We found this man saying he was Christ the King."

Perhaps Pilate was remembering his troubled past, the servitude of his ancestors, some problem, for he hesitated, suspecting a ruse, that the priests were deceiving him. He must have known that I had not preached revolt.

"Are you king of the Jews?" he asked, motioning me to come closer. "Your people have brought you here. What have you done?"

"My kingdom is not of this world."

"Are you a king?"

"I was born to bear witness to the truth."

Pilate shrugged.

"What is truth?" He resumed his seat.

I did not respond.

"What is truth?" he repeated. He waited a little while and then said, looking at me closely: "I find no fault in this man."

Spectators and priests protested. Someone shouted:

"He stirs up the people from here to Galilee. He's a troublemaker. He drove us out of our temple market."

At that moment Pilate may have become aware of my accent or remembered I was born in Nazareth for he ordered me brought to trial before Herod, the local governor. Herod, I thought, the name stunning me as I recalled his crime.

We crossed a bridge, a hostile crowd following; young Herod welcomed me because he had heard of my miracles and wanted me to perform for his benefit. Was I wizard, necromancer, fakir?

I could not speak to this murderer: I envisioned John in prison, waiting, waiting for the liberty that never came. I saw his decapitated head on a tray, displayed for a dancing girl.

Because I could not speak Herod had his men throw a purple robe over my shoulders and place me on a chair. They mocked me, spat on me, and demanded I save myself.

Herod refused to try me and ordered guards to return me to Pontius Pilate. It was then, as we recrossed the bridge where the populace jeered, it was then I attempted to think of home. Something like an actual wall blocked me. All the emptiness of life, the savageness of the wilderness, the enmity of mankind, came into being. I prayed but prayer was useless. A man held my arm or I would have fallen: his sword hit my side.

Peter's
Iyyar 25

Pilate resented a jeering mob and tried to establish order.

He commanded men to assume positions in the Babbatha yard. Calling several priests, he said, shouting at them:

"You have brought this man before me. You say he perverts the people. I find no fault in him. I will punish him and release him."

He sat on his tribunal chair, his wife beside him. Raising his hand he resumed:

"I will free a man. Who will it be? Barabbas? Do you want Barabbas free or Christ? Choose your man."

"Barabbas...Barabbas," the priests shouted, and the crowd repeated his name, a man known for his crimes.

"What shall I do with Jesus?"

"Crucify him...crucify him."

"What has he done?"

The crowd answered: "Crucify him."

Shall I continue this journal? Will others accept my account? Shall I simply destroy these words? As days pass I am able to re-live the sadness. There is a chance to diminish man's cruelty. I take that chance. We are here in this world to make life worthy. We are here to teach others. Teaching is no easier than learning. No one has ever had my vantage point: this permits me to continue.

I searched for a friendly face among the mob...Peter...Mother...Matthew... Clibus...

Barabbas was brought before the judges and liberated with jeers and laughter. He passed by me, a great, tall man. As he walked away I was led to a whipping

post, bound, and lashed with thongs; I was lashed until unconscious. Courage, where was my courage to bear the crucifixion.

I tried to think...

In a barren hall soldiers stripped me and put a filthy robe around me and forced a crown of thorns on my head. Six or eight men confronted me. They mocked me.

"Hail, king of the Jews," they hollered.

Priests appeared and cried: "Crucify him...he calls himself the Son of God. Kill him." Pilate appeared and asked: "Who are you?" I could not speak because of pain.

"Speak to me...don't you realize I have the power to set you free."

I was thinking of Judas.

A Roman officer spoke out: "He's an enemy of Rome...he defies Caesar." "Our emperor is Caesar," a priest shouted.

"Take him away," Pilate said. "He is yours." He took water and washed his hands before the crowd. "I am innocent of the blood of this man," he said.

Again I looked for my disciples but now a centurion in cuirass and armed soldiers, carrying shields, grabbed me and forced me outside. "To the cross," someone said. "To the cross," another repeated.

I was amazed to find myself walking. It isn't far, it isn't far, I told myself.

We descended a stepped path. The bridge lay ahead. People jammed the bridge. We climbed a steep bank, passed houses, trees, rocks. The centurion ordered me to carry the crossbeam. As he compelled me to take the beam he gave me water.

It was nearly noon.

I shouldered the beam, fell, tried again. The officer ordered an onlooker to carry the beam. I heard a priest shout: "If any man wishes to prove the innocence of Jesus, let him speak." His voice, his robe, the beam, the crowd... I can't remember. Yet I remember men selling dates, hawking fruit. I wanted the food of earth, life itself.

My mother broke through the crowd and embraced me. A little farther on I heard Lazarus call. I saw Martha. She was kneeling, reaching toward me. Peter, Luke, Clibus, Mark. I saw. I loved them, their faces like old graven coins.

I saw them all the way to the spot where they laid the cross on the ground. I prayed for courage, strength to endure, as they stripped off my clothes.

Then men pounded a nail through my hand and I was blinded, torn with pain. Then I felt greater pain as they pounded a nail through my legs and then I felt no more pain until I hung on the cross.

I looked and looked but could make out nothing; then I saw two men hanging on crosses beside me. I looked at them and they looked at me. I saw people below me; I heard women and children crying. I tried to speak to them. But as I hung there everything began to move away from me: a great distance swam around me. I thought of a mirage. Someone put a sponge to my mouth. Then I saw my mother, I saw Martha, Lazarus, people I had cured. A soldier shoved his spear into me. I tried to say something... That is all that I remember.

Joseph of Arimathea obtained permission to remove my body from the cross. He and my disciples placed it in his family crypt. He provided a robe and cloth to cover my face. I lay in his tomb, myrrh and aloe about me; there I lay for three days.

*P*eter is a descendant of a nomadic tribe. Euodia, his mother, is a gnarled woman, dark, serious. She and Peter built this house after her husband died. She had had enough of desert privation. Last night she spread a special table for my homecoming: pomegranate juice, melon, cheese, bread, nuts, chromis and another fish, clarias, my favorite. Euodia is an expert with olive oil—perhaps some are nomad recipes. At supper time she accepted me easily; Matthew and Peter were wary, afraid, shy.

While we were eating, Peter said:

"Master, how can it be you were crucified eight days ago... Can you say that you are well?" He brushed his hand over his yellow beard. "I couldn't forget the terror...will you help us understand? When all of us meet will you explain? Is it faith?..."

We were eating at a makeshift table under Peter's olives; it was well after sunset and we felt the quiet of the extensive fields that make Peter's home a retreat.

Matthew, picking at his supper, nervous, kept watching my hands—I knew he was studying the scars.

"I hope you never return to Jerusalem," he exclaimed.

I agreed: I agreed for several reasons: one reason was my desire to send my disciples to remote places, villages, towns.

"Our work is to be carried out among our countrymen while governments interfere."

"We love you...we had nothing to do with the crucifixion," Euodia blurted out.

Love, love after crucifixion is a brilliant but black enigma: it proffers and denies. We know that love helps us forget pain; however I ask myself whether it is evil to forget evil. But I can think of resurrection as a form of love, a love beyond supplication. I take that step and realize that immortality is another form of love.

Desert air pushed in as we finished our meal and we soon felt chilled. I wanted to shed my fatigue by reading but we discussed visiting the spring at Neby. I suggested we leave early if it did not rain during the night and bog the paths. At Neby I wanted to work out a plan for James, Peter and Matthew, if

James joined us. When government cruelty diminishes I want Peter to preach in Rome.

In my bedroom I read *Ecclesiastes*—drowsing at times, aware of my familiar pallet, the good pillow, the candles. I was able to dismiss the imminence of departure. I put it away like a shell under sea grass.

Ecclesiastes meant more to me than weeks ago as I read and re-read passages.

Rain woke me during the night—a pleasant shower smelling like spring. So, we would walk to Neby another day. Here I would be able to go on reading *Ecclesiastes* and Peter's copy of the *Psalms*. When I told Peter that Clibus had found the *Ecclesiastes* scroll on a trip to the upper Nile they were astonished. They had never seen so ancient a scroll.

Peter's
Sivan 5

Judas is dead. He took his own life. His body was found by the daughter of Pontius Pilate. Since he was one of us we have buried him; at his grave a downpour struck us and drove us to a shelter. In a few moments the earth was flooded. I can't recall such rain and thunder.

Judas, born in Gamala, vineyard proprietor, dead at twenty-eight years. As *Ecclesiastes* says: "Woe unto him who is alone when he falls."

Startling, on a hillside, on a hilltop, a contingent of Roman soldiers, a new encampment, white tents in rows, banners, standards, smoke. Shields flash as men drill. Camels are hobbled behind the tent town. We can make out men in half armor, men wearing helmets, men at work shoveling, men erecting a large striped tent.

Is this always glory, power and death?

Peter's—early morning
Sivan 8

Shall we be like trees planted by rivers of water? Shall we mature slowly like the olive? Shall we endure two hundred years? Shall these men replant? They are humble men. Are humble men more or less successful with their lives? These men know ambition and is ambition the safe route? Verily, verily "all is vanity and vexation of spirit," if we listen to *Ecclesiastes*. What will evolve when the silver chord is broken? I have answered these questions in the past but I wish to answer them once more.

Peter's
Sivan 10

Sivan is a beautiful month, a month of subtle changes.

I lay in deep grass yesterday. While I lay in the grass I remembered the fields around Nazareth and I remembered climbing olive trees at harvest time—how we sang and shook down the ripe fruit onto nets.

Mama made the finest olive oil in Papa's oil press, the finest in Nazareth some Nazarenes said. I hurried to fill our baskets... I wanted to gather more than anyone. I never did.

Tomorrow I go to villages and will heal the sick...it is a joy, a joy rather kindred to lying in deep grass in the warm sun.

I have read my journal. I will return it to Matthew's care. Among our disciples he is the most reliable.

Sivan 12

So, as I write with my bronze stylus, I listen to the evening, familiar sounds; through my window I see the Milky Way and the great constellations and I am aware God is affirming his handiwork.

I write very slowly, lingering over each letter, the square letters superior to the old script. I go on listening. The lamp burns steadily. There is no wind. There is gratitude.

Nazareth
Sivan 17

Father has suffered from his imprisonment. His hands tremble. After seeing me on the cross he is unable to believe that I am alive.

I held out my arms to him as we stood in front of our home. He backed away.

"...Father, remember how we visited together at Qumran? Remember that old long-bladed saw, how I repaired its handle three times?

"Mama gave you that shirt at the Feast of Lights..."

He turned and walked away, trembling.

When I was staying at the home of Gehazi, after preaching in the synagogue, after healing, Barabbas appeared. Jamnia is his village and he entered the house of Gehazi without knocking. A great tall hulk, he loomed over me; then he knelt and begged me to accept him.

Dressed in goat's skin, his face and beard wild, he seemed ill, perhaps deranged. I tried to calm him, to reason with him.

"I should have been crucified," he repeated in a hoarse voice.

For a long while we remained together, talking, praying, hoping.

Peter's
Sivan 24

Patience—we need patience.

Going from village to village, town to town, means walking five days, four days, two. It is a five day walk to Nazareth. It is a two day walk to the village of Gehazi. Most walks are pleasant. It can be cold, windy, hot; and when it rains there is seldom any shelter.

Sometimes we travel together; sometimes we walk alone; these days I prefer my solitary walks. I am aware of close communion when alone. Patience, patience...but the calendar moves on: Shevat, Adar, Nisan, Iyyar, Sivan...

will miss Peter's little house, its rough walls, its crooked windows, its clumsy thatched roof. The floors have interested me. He found pieces in some Babylonian structure; he hauled them here in an ox cart. I have come to love this isolation, its olive trees.

Today is a summer's day.

Great clouds, great sky.

Peter sought me out as I sat in the bedroom reading. Again he asked for forgiveness. Kneeling by me he promised he would carry the word... "to Rome, if you wish. Teach me courage, teach me strength, teach me to be wise..."

He and I have worked at the carpenter's bench lately, in Lazarus' shed. It took the three of us to line up a door. Of course it was very old. Laughing, we had to admit our clumsy workmanship.

We are proud that there are more than seventy of us now. I send them out in pairs.

It seems to me I view mankind with a sense of compassion—a constant perception. Mine is a brief, swift looking back: I heal the sick, I renew lives... I remember the hart and the brook...man's insatiable thirst.

Children come and animals come...the ox and the donkey have been friends. A shepherd, I still follow hills, hills of resurrection they may be. Perhaps history may call me a man of righteousness. Perhaps history may not stop. I speak to history. I say, once again:

"Go and teach all nations, baptizing them in the name of the Father, the Son and the Holy Ghost..."

Teach as I have taught...remind them of grace.

Tammuz 11

I leave no tomb, no crypt, no marker.

Finality may not be a friend...

When I leave shall I carry a handful of earth with me?

James, Peter, Matthew, Mark...Mother and Father...Lazarus...Miriam... each one is mine but for how long?

Peter will pick up my sandals and say:

"These were his."

Father will say:

"He helped me make this box."

The Godhead is before me and I struggle with delight and with astonishment.

Tammuz 12

I am entrusting my journal to Matthew. Since we have friends at the synagogue in Capernaum he will leave my journal there.

Verily, verily I say: Fear God and keep His commandments. This is the duty of man.

Farewell Thoughts

I hope these thoughts may be helpful. It is very late and lamplight flickers...

Inside a man of light there is light and with this light he lights the world.

The angels and the prophets will come to you and give you strength.

Blessed are the ones who have heard the Father's word and kept it in truth.

Have you then discovered the beginning so that you ask the end? Where the beginning is, there the end will be.

The kingdom is inside you. When you really understand you will know that you are the son of the living Father. If you do not understand yourself you will be in poverty.

Split wood and I am there. Pick up a stone; there you will find me.

Come to me because my yoke is easy, my lordship gentle. You will find rest.

The kingdom of the Father is spread over the earth and men do not see it.

Blessed are the solitary and the elect; you shall find the kingdom because you have come from it and you shall go there again.

I say, whenever one is one he will be filled with light, but whenever he is divided he will be filled with darkness.

Love your brother as your own soul. Guard him as the apple of your eye.

There will be days when you seek and you will not find me.

NOTE:

These logia appear for the first time in a journal.
They are from the 4th century Coptic book,
The Gospel According to Thomas,
discovered in Hammadi, Egypt,
quoted through the courtesy
of the translator, Dr. Ray Rummers,
Chairman, Department of English, Baylor University.

ABOUT THE AUTHOR

*P*aul Alexander Bartlett (1909-1990) was a writer and artist, born in Moberly, Missouri, and educated at Oberlin College, the University of Arizona, the Academia de San Carlos in Mexico City, and the Instituto de Bellas Artes in Guadalajara. His work can be divided into three categories: He is the author of many novels, short stories, and poems; second, as a fine artist, his drawings, illustrations, and paintings have been exhibited in more than forty one-man shows in leading galleries, including the Los Angeles County Museum, the Atlanta Art Museum, the Bancroft Library, the Richmond Art Institute, the Brooks Museum, the Instituto-Mexicano-Norteamericano in Mexico City, and many other galleries; and, third, he devoted much of his life to the most comprehensive study of the haciendas of Mexico that has been undertaken. More than 350 of his pen-and-ink illustrations of the

haciendas and more than one thousand hacienda photographs make up the Paul Alexander Bartlett Collection held by the Nettie Lee Benson Latin American Collection of the University of Texas, and form part of a second diversified collection held by the American Heritage Center of the University of Wyoming, which also includes an archive of Bartlett's literary work, fine art, and letters.

Paul Alexander Bartlett's fiction has been commended by many authors, among them Pearl Buck, Ford Madox Ford, John Dos Passos, James Michener, Upton Sinclair, Evelyn Eaton, and many others. He was the recipient of many grants, awards, and fellowships, from such organizations as the Leopold Schepp Foundation, the Edward MacDowell Association, the New School for Social Research, the Huntington Hartford Foundation, the Montalvo Foundation, and the Carnegie Foundation.

His wife, Elizabeth Bartlett, a widely published poet, is the author of seventeen published books of poetry, numerous poems, short stories, and essays published in leading literary quarterlies and anthologies, and, as the founder of Literary Olympics, Inc., is the editor of a series of multi-language volumes of international poetry that honor the work of outstanding contemporary poets.

Paul and Elizabeth's son, Steven, edited and designed this volume.

Christ's Journal

was set in Garamond type by Autograph Editions. The typeface is named after Claude Garamond (c. 1480-1561), a French type designer and publisher and the world's first commercial typefounder. Garamond's contribution to the history of typesetting was substantial. He perfected the design of Roman type: The fonts that he cut beginning in 1531 were recognized as possessing a superior grace and clarity, so much so that Garamond's fonts influenced European printing for the next century and a half.

It is interesting to note that Garamond type is the evolutionary ancestor of the type used to print the first official copies of the Declaration of Independence. In the 1730s, Englishman William Caslon refined Garamond's version of Aldine roman, the well-balanced typeface became popular, and was introduced to the American colonies by Benjamin Franklin.

Despite his considerable contribution to the evolution of typography, Garamond was not a successful businessman and he died in poverty.

During the past five centuries, so many variations of Garamond's type designs have been created that the phrase 'Garamond type' has come to be used loosely, with little memory remaining of its history.

www.ingramcontent.com/pod-product-compliance
Lightning Source LLC
Chambersburg PA
CBHW021130130626
46554CB00002B/939